Christmas Can Be Murder

A Chaplain Merriman Christian Cozy Mystery

Jacob Lee & Liz Dodwell

www.mix-booksonline.com

Table of Contents

One

It's amazing to some people that it can be warm enough to ride a motorcycle in early December, but here in Alpena, Arkansas, it's not all that uncommon. Oh, the weather isn't perfect every day, of course, but it's pretty nice some of the time. It's one of the reasons Nervy and I decided to move here when it came time for me to retire.

Now don't get me wrong, even though the days in December can be fairly warm, when it's dark and after ten p.m. it starts to get a bit chilly. When you ride a motorcycle in that kind of weather, you learn quickly that the only way to do so is fast, because you want to get quickly to wherever you're going, get off and get inside someplace warm. I was zipping along Old Cemetery Road at about forty miles an hour, about as fast as Clark Rodgers, our police chief, is gonna let me get away with, when I caught a glimpse of something coming out of the woods on the right.

At first, I thought it was a deer, but then I realized it was a person, so I slammed on the brakes and slid to a stop. I threw down the kickstand and jumped off as the figure collapsed onto the roadway, but I knew it was too late as soon as I got to her. It was a young mother I had seen around town and even invited to church, and she was slick with blood.

I whipped out my phone and called 911, but I knew that sound as the death rattle hit. She was gone, and as I told the emergency dispatcher where to find her body, I leapt to my feet and ran through the woods to where I knew she lived in a house near that spot. This woman had a three-year-old son, and I was terrified that something equally horrible may have happened to the child.

I found the kitchen door standing wide open and raced inside. There was blood everywhere, and I could see a trail of it where she had obviously staggered out the door. Inside, there was a pool of blood and signs of a struggle — the coffee pot was broken on the floor, a skillet was up under the table, chairs were overturned. I could tell that she had fought for her life, and it broke my heart that she had lost, but I was most concerned about her son. I searched hurriedly through the house and found the boy, thankfully sound asleep and unaware of what had happened. I called 911 again and told the dispatcher to let Clark Rodgers know where I was and why, then let my curiosity get the better of me and began to poke around.

Two

Perhaps I'd better back up a bit and introduce myself. I'm Dexter Merriman, but my friends call me Dex. A few people call me Chappy, which is a reference to the fact that I had been a Chaplain in the US Army, retired eighteen months ago as a Lieutenant Colonel. I had a little more than thirty years in, so with better than sixty thousand a year to live on, we figured it would be a great place to spend our twilight years together, a place for our son to bring his kids for visits, things like that.

My wife Nervy and I had bought the house in Alpena back in 2012, after passing through the town on a trip to Branson, Missouri with some friends who had retired a few years before. We'd fallen in love with the little town as we drove through it, and since we had a couple of extra days left on our leave, we'd decided to look it over before we went back. As we walked along the old streets, some of them actually with old brick showing through the pavement in places, there was such a sense of peace and hominess that we both felt drawn to settle there when I retired, so we stopped in at the town's only realtor's office.

"Hi," said the thin man who sat behind the only desk in the one-room office. "I'm Max Woolcott, what can I do for you nice folks today?"

We told him we were just thinking about the town as a potential retirement location, and that was all it took. We heard all about what a wonderful community it was, with only four hundred-odd residents who lived there year round, a surrounding countryside that boasted numerous chicken and turkey farms and a delightful tourist trade because of so many craftspeople who lived there. The main street, as we'd already seen, was a line of craft and specialty shops, which was one of the very things we'd loved so much about it. Nervy and I were both inveterate bargain hunters and craft lovers, so we envisioned many years of browsing the shops and hanging out with the locals.

Max was so easy to talk to that, before we knew it, we were in his car and on our way to look at houses. We saw a couple of them that were small, but since we were anticipating many future visits from our grandchildren, we passed those up. We looked at a nice, modern ranch style house next, but Nervy thought it was too fancy for us, so we passed it up as well, and went on to the next, and that was the one we both knew was home.

It was a nice little three bedroom bungalow about two miles out on the south edge of town, with a garage out back that was attached to the house by a short, covered walkway, and some big, beautiful oak trees scattered around the yard. I had the instant thought that I could see myself building a hot rod in the garage, and pushing Ben in a swing that hung from one of the trees, and Nervy said the kitchen felt like it was made specifically for her. The house was empty and was part of an estate that had been inherited by a young couple off in California, so we got to really spend time looking it over. I went into the basement and inspected the foundation, then climbed up into the attic and looked for any signs of roof leaks. Max stood there and smiled as we did his job for him, and before we left there, we had made up our minds to make an offer on the place. I'd seen some work that it would need, so I offered a few thousand below what the sellers were asking, and we hadn't even made it back to Fort Benning before Max called to tell us it was accepted. We got our financing approved a few days later, and began making monthly payments on the home we would never get to live in together.

You see, life doesn't always go the way you expect it to go, and it doesn't even pay a lot of attention to the plans we make, for that matter. Nervy—her name was Minerva, but one of her friends had given her that nickname long before we met, and it fit her, so I got in the habit of using it, too—Nervy would have loved living in this little town, with all its quirky residents and quaint, historic buildings. Yes, she would have loved it. Unfortunately, she died just a few months before we had planned to make our break with the Army.

It was a freak accident, so freakish that for a while, there were a few people who thought I'd murdered my wife. Heck, even I thought so for a while but, there. You see, she got up early every morning to make me coffee and breakfast, that was just her way. That last morning, she'd gone into the kitchen to start the coffee, and I guess she reached into the dishwasher to get out a cup, but she left it open part way. I don't know what happened next, but I heard a crash and a scream, and I leapt out of bed and went running to the kitchen to find her laying on the floor, with one of our big butcher knives stuck in her side.

The knife had been in the rack on the door of the dishwasher; I know, because I'd put it there the night before, and I didn't even think about the fact that she was always telling me to make sure I always put them in blade down.

9

For some idiotic reason, though, I always got it backwards and put them in blade up, and when she slipped or whatever that made her fall onto the door of the dishwasher, it had been sticking straight up and gone straight in.

I grabbed the phone and called the Post's emergency services while I tried to stop the bleeding, but the knife had pierced her heart. I held her while she died, and though she couldn't manage to speak, her eyes told me over and over again that she loved me, and that she'd be waiting for me. The paramedics and MP's arrived too late, and found me holding her and sobbing on my bloody kitchen floor, crying that I had accidentally killed my wife.

After a month long investigation and a coroner's inquest, I was cleared and her death was ruled an accident. She had slipped on a wet spot on the floor, probably from water she'd spilled out of the coffee pot, and fallen onto the flatware rack in the dishwasher door. That damned knife was pointed upward, and at just the right angle to slide between her ribs…

Our family and friends had come to comfort me in my time of grief, and Chance, our son, came and helped me get the arrangements made and such. I took an emergency leave and made it through the funeral somehow, but then, after everyone else had gone, I walked into my living room and stood there for a few minutes, just staring around me, and suddenly all of the emotions I'd been holding back flooded free.

"How dare You!" I screamed at God. "How dare You take her from me like this! How dare You leave me to face the rest of this life alone? What kind of God are You, that would reward my years of service to You this way?"

I fell to my knees, and it was at that point that I began to question my faith. If the God that I had served so long could treat me like this, after I'd done all I could to serve Him in the best way I knew how, then was He ever real at all? How could a God of Love allow such things to happen?

For the next two weeks, that was about all I could think of, and finally I decided that I could not continue to serve such a God. When the inquest finally cleared me of any wrongdoing, I filed for retirement, and when it was approved, I mustered out as quickly as I could and arrived in Alpena only three months after Nervy's death. It still hurt, every single day, and I had come to understand what people had meant all through the years, when they would tell me that it felt like the one they'd lost was still with them. I talked to Nervy as if she was still right there beside me, and sometimes I could even imagine her responses. It made her loss a little more bearable, and I was grateful for it.

We'd had a car, but when I retired and moved, I had decided to start over completely, so I sold everything we'd had except for a few things that were just too precious to give up. One of those was the old 1948 Harley Panhead that I'd found in a garage during a rummage sale, and painstakingly restored over eight years of Saturdays. I'd always had a motorcycle, and the Harley was one that both Nervy and I loved to ride, so much so that, once it was finished, I'd sold the Honda Goldwing we'd used for years. When everything else was sold or packed, I shipped all of what was left to Arkansas, but then I climbed onto that big hog and rode it every bumpy mile from Fort Benning to Alpena. There were moments on that ride when I would have sworn that Nervy was on the queen seat behind me, her hair blowing out from under her helmet, and a smile spread across her face.

Moving didn't help. The depression I'd fallen into followed me to Arkansas, and I found myself refusing to pray, refusing to do much of anything other than sit at home and mope around the house. Two months after I'd moved in, I was still living out of boxes and eating nothing that I couldn't heat up in the microwave, and Chance finally decided it was time for an Intervention. He and Lindsay and Ben showed up on a Friday night, and I managed to put on a smile until we got the boy to bed and fast asleep.

Then I poured out my heart. Chance had followed in his old man's footsteps, and gone to Seminary. He was the pastor of a small but exciting Baptist church in Olney, Illinois, only about a six-hour drive from Alpena, and he asked me to pray with him about what was happening with me.

"What?" I asked. "Can't a man question his own faith? Haven't you ever questioned your own?"

"Yeah, I have," he admitted. "As I recall, it was a few times during school, and then more than once after I started preaching, and it was you who always reminded me that there was one thing we could be certain of, and that was the fact that no matter what else we might believe, there is still the one incontrovertible fact that can't be denied—and that is that when the sun rose on the third day after Jesus was crucified, the tomb was empty. If the God we serve can raise Jesus from the dead, then He's the God who can help us to overcome any crisis of faith."

He sighed and put a hand on my shoulder, while Lindsay held onto my free hand. "Dad, I understand," he

Jacob Lee

said. "Remember, I lost my mother in this acc
Jesus is still there, and He still loves us, and He
for us to pray so that He can move in our lives."

I tried, I really did. I prayed, but it seem
prayers weren't going as high as the ceiling, an I didn't
know how to make them reach any higher. On Saturday, I
spent the day with all three of them, and they got me out of
the house for a while in the afternoon. We went to a few of
the craft shops, and then had lunch at a little place that was
simply called "the Diner." After that, I took Ben to the park
for a bit, just the two of us, while Chance and Lindsay visited
a shop that specialized in baby items.

My grandson didn't know what to think of how I was
acting, but it was he who actually brought me out of it. I
remember that I was on the See-Saw with him, carefully
boosting him into the air, when he looked at me with that
innocence that only a child can truly know and said,
"Grandpa, it's okay. I know why God took Grandma home."

I stopped the See-Saw with him up in the air, and felt
something stir inside me, for I had just asked that question
silently in my heart — Why, God, why did you take her home,
and leave me here?

I smiled up at Ben. "Oh, you do, do you?" I asked, and
I could hear the dryness in my voice, the fear of what he
might say.

He nodded. "Yes," he said. "God just needed another
angel, and Grandma was the best one He could find, so He
took her home to Heaven so He could give her her wings.
She'll watch over all of us, now."

But, as I said, that was almost a year and a half ago.
Time had passed, and wounds had healed, and I was among

the living once again. These days, I attended church at the local First Baptist, where Brother Freddy, who was seventy-five years old and whose very first words to me were, "I love you," preached sermons that saw souls saved often, and where they had an average of six baptisms a month. If there was one thing that helped me recover my own faith, I'd have to say it was letting that old fellow stomp my toes, which he did every time he got to preaching on long hair (mine is down to below my shoulders, now).

I had also decided it was time to return to serving God, so I approached the Sheriff's Captain who ran the local county detention center about starting a jailhouse ministry. As a former military Chaplain, I was well versed in the practices of most Christian denominations, so he agreed, and I began holding a service there on Sunday afternoons, and coming in twice a week to speak to inmates who wanted some spiritual counseling. It kept me busy, and Chance and Lindsay were happy to see that I was able to smile and pray again.

Life was getting back to where it should be, and I was enjoying it again. I'd been the beneficiary on Nervy's life insurance, of course, and it was large enough that I paid off the house and put a hefty chunk into trust for Ben and his year-old sister, Marie. If there were more grandchildren, they'd be added as beneficiaries to the trust, as well, but Chance and Lindsay swore that two was more than enough. Heck, Chance had been such a little hellion that I was glad we only had one, so I could understand.

Things were good. I'd been shanghaied by the town's Parade Committee into playing Santa this year, which is because I look a lot like him — long white hair and beard, and a belly that knows what it means to "jiggle with laughter," so on that particular evening, I had ridden over to the dress shop, where Naoma Brodrick, the lady who heads the committee, had arranged for the Santa Suit to be fitted to me. I'd somehow made it through two hours of trying it on and taking it off, and was on my way home.

Three

OK, now where was I? Oh, yeah; in the dead woman's house, making sure her little boy stayed safe, and nosing around a bit.

Chief of Police Clark Rodgers showed up about fifteen minutes later, and I knew he was mad the moment I saw him.

"Dex," he said, "what do you think you're doing? You found the victim and called it in, and then left the scene, and now I find you here in the middle of a crime scene, contaminating the crap out of it! I would have thought you were smarter than that!" He stormed past me into the kitchen, and began ordering men with him to take pictures and check this and that and other police-type things that he probably understood no better than I did.

Don't look at me like that, he was chief of police in a town of four hundred people; do you really think they look for things like a degree in forensic technologies? Clark was elected to the job because half the town recalls his winning touchdowns when he was quarterback of the high school football team!

"I'm here," I said calmly, "because I knew that poor woman was dead, and I recognized her as Brenda Hawley. Brenda's little boy has played with my grandson at the park a couple of times, so I instantly thought about him and ran here to make sure he was okay."

"That's a job for the police, Chaplain," he said, making my title seem like an insult at that moment.

"Well, then, I'll ask you to forgive me, Chief," I said, giving back as good as I got in the insult department. "My main concern at that moment was for the living, rather than the dead, and for the record, yes, I'm smart enough not to touch anything here. I saw that the boy was asleep, looked through the house to be sure the killer wasn't still here, and then stood right here where I could hear the boy if he woke up and started crying, and waited for you. Is that good enough?"

I could see his anger deflate a bit, as he was forced to agree that I'd done the right thing under the circumstances. "Yeah, okay," he said, "makes sense, I guess, and I'd rather you be here with the kid than anyone else I can think of who might have been involved. And speaking of involved, what are you even doing out at this time of night? I saw that motorbike of yours over by the body; isn't it a little cold to be out for a moonlight ride?"

I nodded. "Yeah, it would be, except that I'm doing Santa in the parade this Saturday, and the committee wanted me at a suit fitting tonight. You can check with Naoma Brodrick or Selma Lender at the dress shop, I was with the two of them all evening."

He wrote that down in a little notebook he took from a pocket. "I will," he said. "How did you come upon all this?"

I gave a shrug and nodded towards where I'd left my motorcycle, back through the woods. "I was on the way home from the fitting. Cemetery Road is the quickest way."

He harrumphed. "You mean it's the best way to go if you don't want me to catch you speeding, right? Okay, so you found Brenda laying there in the road?"

18

"Nope," I said. "She came out of the woods at the side of the road, and scared me half to death. I managed not to hit her as I stopped, but by the time I got off the bike, she was falling. Dark as it was, I could tell by the feel and the smell that she was covered in blood, and when I heard her breathe her last, I thought of little Colton. I knew she lived right over here, so I ran as fast as I could to make sure he was all right, and thank God, I found him safe."

Clark wrote all that down, and asked me again if I'd touched anything. I replied that the only thing I had touched in the house was the light switch in Colton's room, and he said I'd need to come to his office the next morning to make an official statement.

I looked around at Clark's two Barney Fife clones, and it occurred to me that they weren't going to do much in the way of crime scene investigation. I glanced at their chief's face, which was pretty pale, and said, "I'm sure you saw the nicks in the kitchen floor, right? Where it looks like someone was stabbing at someone on the floor, and kept missing?"

Clark looked down at the floor and his eyes went wide, but then he glared at me. "Yeah," he said, "I saw that, and I saw that the knife block is missing a knife, too. Don't try to do my job for me, Dex, it's a little out of your department."

"True," I said. "Seems kind of odd to me, though, that the knife that's missing from the block is the big French Chef, with a wide, sort of thick blade, but the nicks in the floor are tiny. They look more like the work of a filet knife, don't you think?" I pointed at the block again, and the filet knife that was right in its proper place.

Clark looked at it, then back at me, and said, "My office, tomorrow morning, Dex. Now, get out of here."

I got. I went back to my bike and got there just as the county Medical Examiner was loading up poor Brenda's body, but other than whispering a prayer, there wasn't much I could do. I climbed on the Harley and headed for home, let myself in, then washed the blood off of me the best I could and went to bed. The blood all over Brenda, and then all over me, had brought back some pretty rough memories of the morning Nervy died, so it took me a little while to get to sleep.

I woke to find Baggins on my chest, kneading it with his front paws, and I was glad that I had put on my thick sweatshirt before I'd slipped into bed. Without it, his claws could do me some damage, and had resulted in him getting some frequent flyer miles, when the sudden surprise of claws digging into sensitive flesh had caused me to react by flinging my arms about, but it hadn't broken him of it.

Baggins was my cat. His curly fur, and the fact that it seems to be thickest on his feet, reminded me of a Hobbit, which is how he got his name. He'd shown up on my doorstep one morning meowing at me, and I almost thought I could translate his meows as Meriadoc Brandybuck's line from The Lord Of The Rings, "Where's my bed and brrrreakfast?" Kneading was simply his way of saying, "Hey, Human! It's time to feed me!"

I could push him off, in which case he'd be back in fifteen minutes. I could ignore him, in which case he'd keep digging deeper until the sweatshirt wasn't thick enough; or I could get my lazy blessed assurance out of bed and make him some breakfast, which struck me as the path of wisdom in this case. I gently shoved him aside, then rolled over and let my feet fall into my slippers and headed for the kitchen.

Baggins knew where I was going, and beat me there, walking figure eights around his bowls. I filled one with his favorite dry cat food, then rinsed out the other and gave him fresh water. Once that was all taken care of, his meows seemed to say that I was free to consider my own breakfast needs, so I put on a pot of coffee and waited until it was far enough along that I could get a cup, then popped a frozen breakfast burrito into the microwave and told it to get hot in a hurry.

When both were on the table in front of me, I sat down and started thinking about the events of the night before. Between the similarities between Brenda's and Nervy's deaths, and my natural concern for the little boy, I hadn't really slept all that much, and I was having trouble getting my mind off of them.

Yeah, yeah, I know—Clark told me to stay out of it, but sometimes a Shepherd just has to worry about sheep, even if they aren't in his own flock, y'know? I ate my burrito, told myself I didn't need the second one my appetite was begging for, and wondered if it was too early to go to the station. Maybe, if I went about it just the right way, I could get some information out of Barney Fife—I mean, out of Mike Miller, the only other full time officer the town had.

I was just sitting there, thinking about it all, when I heard something outside, and I saw Baggins raise his head and look at the back door. A second later, there was a knock on it, which was surprising since almost no one ever bothered to come to my house. I wondered who it could be, but the only way to find out was to get up and answer it, so I did.

"Well, are ye gon' let me in, or just stand there gawkin' at me?" The woman who asked me that question was one of the more, shall we say, colorful of the local folk, and that was saying a lot! She was known as 'Crazy Maisy,' and is somewhat famous on a wide scale for her homemade remedies and such, things she sells in the local monthly flea market during tourist season. I particularly like her fire cider, a blend of things like peppers, horseradish, garlic, ginger and other spices, with honey. Around this time of year, there isn't much that can warm you up after a chill like a hot toddy with a shot of rye whiskey, another shot of honey liqueur and about four ounces of fire cider! I haven't had a cold since I discovered the stuff, and it'd take an act of congress to take it away from me! I even added a dash of it to my coffee on cold mornings!

Maisy lives in an old trailer out in the woods not far from town, one of those old round-cornered, silvery ones that was originally meant to be used for traveling. I've been out to it a couple of times, and if you ask me, it's probably time to haul it to the scrap yard, but she calls it home. Somewhere in her yard, you could probably find just about any type of antique gadget you might wish for, and there's an old school bus out back of the trailer that is literally packed full of furniture and dishes and toys and God alone knows what else. I'd bet the contents would fetch a small fortune at a decent antique auction, but Maisy won't hear of any such thing. When anyone comes around asking to look at her treasures, she'll smile and dig through things with them all day long, asking five or ten dollars for each item no matter how big or small or old, or even what it's made of. I shudder when I think of the priceless antiques that people have happily bought for far, far less than they should have paid.

But that's Maisy. She isn't all that interested in money.

I stood aside and allowed her into the house, ignoring the pungent odor that goes everywhere Maisy goes, like a shadow that only your nose can detect. It isn't actually unpleasant, and it isn't body odor; it's a combination of all of the spices and oils and such that she works with in making her various decoctions, but it certainly makes its presence known.

"Good morning, Maisy," I said. "Would you like some coffee?"

She stomped over to my kitchen table and sat down in my chair. "Nah, I don't need no coffee. I come by to tell ye somethin' 'bout that dead woman ye found last night!"

I stared at her, wondering how on earth she could know anything about Brenda Hawley's murder, or my involvement in it, but this was Crazy Maisy; there were stories about her that made one think of clairvoyance and old Ozark Mountain witchcraft. I was flustered, and sat down opposite her and took a big swig out of my own cup.

I was about to ask her what she had to say when Baggins suddenly hopped up into her lap. He's not normally very sociable, and it struck me that he would take to her so easily, but then again, he was a cat; if Maisy were some kind of witch, then cats would be part of her world, wouldn't they?

I mentally slapped myself for thinking like that, and smiled at my guest. "If you know something about that poor woman's murder, Maisy, you should go to the police. Why would you come to me?"

She scowled. "I got no faith in police, and Clark Rodgers ain't got no business wearin' a badge, nohow! Many's a time my old Pop caught him stealin' from us when he was a boy! And I ain't got much believin' in God, either, but I can see when someone be a man of integrity, and ye be one of the best at that, so I can trust ye to do as right!"

Her odd, back hills way of talking always amused me, but I tried my best not to let it show. "Do as right about what?" I asked, and she stopped stroking Baggins to look up at me and squint one eye until it was almost closed.

"I might just be knowin' who the killer be!" She said with an air of importance, and while that wasn't quite what I expected her to say, I wasn't completely taken aback.

"Then you really should go to the police, Maisy," I insisted, but once again she shook her head. I sighed, and said, "Okay, then, go on."

She gave me her one-eyed squint again. "Was five years gone, she came to me one night, wantin' a potion to help her get with child. Now, I've knowed Brenda Hawley all her life, but I hadn't heard nothin' about her gettin' married, so I asked, and she said she wasn't, so I told her I would not help her bring a child into the world, and it not have a family! Too much o' that these days as it is!"

I raised an eyebrow, surprised that her morals were so strong on that point. "Maisy," I said, "I'm impressed. That's a very commendable thing to do, and I'm proud of you, but what has it got to do with the poor girl's murder?"

She snapped both her eyes open and glared at me. "Well, and I'm a-comin' to that, can't ye keep your pants on?

So, anyway, one of the things I always need is evening primrose, and there's a big patch of it in the clearing out back a ways from Brenda's house. I go out to gather it in the evening, of course, and more than once when I was there did I see a man a-sneakin' away from her back door to the house next door!" She narrowed one eye again, and nodded once, briskly. "And was again yesterday evening, as I went to gather some of the roots before the big frost that's comin' next week, that I seen the same feller sneaking away again!"

I'm sure that both my eyebrows went up, then, and I was about to ask her if she knew the man, but she stood up, dumping Baggins onto the floor without warning, and walked out the back door without another word. I called after her twice, but she kept going as if she couldn't hear a word, and finally I shook my head and poured myself another cup of coffee.

Four

I puttered around the house for a couple of hours, trying to tell myself that Maisy was probably full of baloney, and that even if she had seen a man leaving Brenda's house, it likely meant nothing at all.

However, a morbid curiosity has often been my downfall. Back in the Army, I used to ask other Chaplains to cover for me on the days I was scheduled to take Catholic confessions, simply because I'd go nuts trying to figure out who some of the people were who told me their secrets. The Confessional is supposed to be sacred, so for me to even wonder about such things was a sin. Unfortunately, that's how bad my nosiness could be, and I could feel it getting its fur up on this murder case.

I knew I should call Clark and tell him what Maisy had said, but then they'd want to talk to her, and she'd end up mad at me. I finally decided to just take a look at Brenda's neighbor's house, and see if I could get a sense of whether it was important. Something about Maisy's words, and the way she'd said them, wasn't sitting well with me, and I just felt the need to do something.

I got on the Harley and rode out toward Brenda's, then slowed as I turned onto her road. I wanted to look like I was just riding by, not even a little bit curious about the houses on the street, and I'm sure I was failing miserably, but there was no help for it.

I noticed immediately that the houses were not very close together, and that sort of surprised me. Not living there, I'd always had the impression that they were closer than they were, but that was probably because I would have ridden past them rather quickly. Everything looks close together when you're passing it at forty or fifty miles an hour, but when you slow down, you can see the actual distance between the houses, or telephone poles, or what have you. In this case, there was probably a good hundred and fifty yards between houses, and there were only four of them on this whole stretch of road. Brenda's was next to last as you approached the opposite end from where I was at.

A trash truck turned onto the street from the other end, coming off of Old Cemetery Road, where I'd found Brenda the night before, and an idea hit me. I stopped the bike near Brenda's house and waited until it got to the pile in front of her place, then walked over to talk to the two men who were tossing stuff into the truck.

"Hi," I said, "I'm Dex Merriman, I'm with the local Christmas toy drive. You guys didn't see a box of toys set out here, did you? This lady said she had some toys to donate." I sent up a silent prayer for forgiveness for the little white lie.

They looked at each other, and then one of them looked at me. "No, sir," he said, "haven't seen any toys. I guess you heard she got killed last night, right? It was all over the radio this morning."

I nodded sadly. "Yeah, I heard, that's kind of why I rode by. I was supposed to pick them up this morning, and I was hoping maybe she'd set them outside for me, but they've got the whole house taped off for the investigation, so I don't even want to try to get up there. If it wasn't out here by the trash, I guess I should just write it off."

The guy nodded. "Yeah, I guess so," he said. "Really sorry about that. We sorta knew her, and she was a nice lady, always polite and friendly. Such a sweetheart."

His partner laughed. "Yeah, she was great. Bo, here, he had a crush on her."

Bo grinned. "Why not? She wasn't like a lot of people, who think garbage men are someone to look down on, know what I mean? It was a real shame, her getting stabbed to death in her own kitchen like that, y'know?"

I smiled and nodded. "I do," I said. "Some of them look down on long haired motorcycle riders, too, believe me!"

They laughed at that, and I glanced at the space between the houses. There was a hedgerow on each side of Brenda's house, and to go from either one of the houses that neighbored hers would mean climbing through the hedge. It struck me that getting all scratched up by the piney bristles was something you wouldn't likely do unless you were trying to be sneaky and not be seen.

"Yeah, it's a shame about Miss Hawley," I said again. "I wonder if she was close to her neighbors? Do you know either of them?"

Bo turned and pointed at one of the houses. "Old couple lives there," he said, and I caught the scent of some fairly strong alcohol on his breath. He turned and pointed at the other house. "That one, he's a single guy. He's got money, he's one of them people thinks he's better'n everyone else."

I took notice of the house he was pointing at, and saw that he was probably right about the guy having money. I spotted some landscaping that I knew must have cost a pretty penny, and a fairly large bronze fountain stood in his front yard. I knew, because Nervy had always wanted a small bronze fountain, that they were far from cheap.

In my years as a Chaplain, I had been called on many times to counsel soldiers, both male and female, who had been the victims of one form of abuse or another, and one of the common denominators of many of the stories I heard from female soldiers was that the abuser was often financially well off, or seemed to be. In psychology courses, I had learned that wealth tends to reduce compassion, meaning that people who consider themselves to be fairly well off have a tendency to be cruel to people they consider beneath their own social status; that would explain the neighbor's disdain for the garbage men, but if he were consorting with Brenda, might he also have looked down on her? Domestic abuse and rape is just as prevalent among the affluent as it is among the poor.

There didn't seem to be anything more to learn from the two men, so I thanked them and got back on the Harley. I rode down to the police station and went inside looking for Chief Rodgers. Mike Miller was behind the desk, and he found my statement and gave it to me to sign, then told me that the chief was out, working on the murder case.

"Oh, well," I said, "I think I may have stumbled across some additional evidence. I had a visit this morning from Crazy Maisy, and she told me that on a lot of evenings when she was out gathering herbs back behind Brenda's house, she saw a man sneaking through the hedges from Brenda's house to the one next door. And she said she saw him again last night, probably not long before the murder. Maisy didn't want to come in to the station, but I felt like this was something important that the chief should hear."

Mike grinned at me. "Yeah, well, we all know Maisy," he said. "She's a weird old bat, isn't she?"

I kept a grin on my face, even though what I really wanted to do was lecture the young man about respect for his elders and the dangers of judging others. "Oh, I kind of like her," I said. "She's definitely a character, that much I'll agree with. Be sure and tell Clark about it, and give him my best. I'm going to go and see if I can find out where Brenda's son is staying, I'd like to check up on the boy, being a man of God. It's a terrible thing, to lose a parent, especially when you only have one, and it seems even worse at Christmas time. I don't think anyone even knows who the boy's father is, do they?"

Mike shrugged his shoulders. "I sure don't," he said, "and the way everybody else talks, I think it was some kind of big secret she was keeping. The boy's over at his grandpa's house, that's where they took him. Gavin, Brenda's daddy, him and his new wife took him when they found out about her being dead, last night."

I smiled and nodded. "Ah, yes, he would be next of kin." I didn't know Gavin Hawley, but a lot of local speculation seemed to paint a picture of him as a sort of home-grown Al Capone, here in Boone County. If we had a local gangster, that would be him. I had heard stories that he was involved in everything from chop shops to drug dealing and even money laundering. "Well, be sure and pass that on to Clark, and tell him I'll see him again soon." I started to turn away, and then stopped and looked back at Mike. "You, um, wouldn't happen to have her father's address, would you?"

Mike nodded. "Sure enough," he said, checking a note on his desk. "He lives over in Long Creek, right where

County Road 56 hits Highway 412. Big monster of a house that's shaped like a barn. You can't miss it."

I nodded my thanks and turned to walk out the door. Something cold and wet landed on my nose, and I realized that the sky was spitting snow. That would be great for the Saturday parade, but it wasn't so wonderful for riding a Harley. It wasn't falling heavy, yet, and the road would be warm enough that it wouldn't stick, so I got on the bike, buttoned my coat and rode out of town towards Long Creek. I wanted to get there before Clark found out I was sticking my nose where he didn't figure it belonged.

Mike was right, and I had no trouble finding the huge house that not only was shaped like a barn but, rather obviously, had actually been one at some time in the past. The stories about Gavin having millions of dollars seemed to have some truth to them, for converting an old barn to a three story marvel of a mansion as beautiful as the one I stood before, would certainly take quite a lot of the stuff. He could probably afford it, though; Hawley Construction was a big name around the area, and had been winning a lot of major building contracts for several years. They'd built everything from the new City Hall in Harrison to some resort hotels up in Branson, Missouri, a half hour away to the north.

I knocked on the door, and a young blonde woman answered a moment later. She was obviously either drunk or stoned, and since it was only lunch time, I was taken slightly aback.

"Hi, there," I said. "I'm Chaplain Dexter Merriman, I'm the one who found Brenda last night and went to check on the little boy. I understand he's here staying with his grandfather? I just wanted to stop by and see how he's doing."

The young woman shrugged her shoulders and stepped aside to let me enter. Instantly, I heard a child crying somewhere upstairs, and a man shouting for the young woman to "go and shut that brat up!" The woman looked toward the sound of his voice, then glanced back at me and giggled.

Alarmed, and worried about the boy, I pushed past the girl and went toward the sound of the crying. It was coming through a closed door at the top of the first flight of stairs; I opened it to find the child standing in the middle of the room, sucking his thumb and crying in what sounded like pure terror, and it was obvious he had wet himself. The young woman caught up with me, yelling at me to stop and get out, but when she saw the boy standing there with his pants obviously soaked, she seemed to forget me completely and began screaming obscenities at him, then raised her hand as if to strike him, and I had all I could take.

I caught her wrist and pushed her back without even thinking about what I was doing, then snatched the boy up into my arms just as Brenda's father, Gavin, came rushing up the stairway. He had a look of a heavy drinker himself, and was definitely not sober, nor was he a small man. He blocked the doorway and glared at me.

"You want to tell me just what in the Sam Hill is going on, here?" he asked. "Just who the heck are you, and what are you doing in my house?"

The young woman turned to Gavin, and he put an arm around her and pulled her close to him. I suddenly remembered what Mike had said, about Gavin and his new wife taking the little boy in, and realized that this must be the new wife he mentioned.

"Baby," she said, "I don't know who he is, he just pushed right past me and came running in here!"

"It's all right, Tiffany," Gavin said. It struck me that he was probably at least as old as I was, if not older, while Tiffany appeared to be in her late teens or very early twenties, at the most. I decided to ignore her, and speak to Gavin.

"Mr. Hawley," I began, "I'm Chaplain Merriman, the man who found your daughter when she was killed last night, and took care of your grandson until the police arrived. Now, I'm not trying to stick my nose in where it doesn't belong, but it appears to me that the boy is in your way, that he's perhaps more responsibility than you need to be dealing with right now. If you like, I could probably make a phone call and arrange for someone to take care of him for now so that you won't have to…"

That was as far as I got, before Gavin let go of his wife and took a step toward me. "You listen to me," he said, threateningly. "That boy is my grandson, and I will do with him as I darn well please. Ain't you or nobody else gonna come in here and try to tell me how to take care of my grandson! You understand that, preacher man?" He stomped his way to me and reached out to take the little boy, who was by this time screaming in what I took to be abject terror, and I turned to try to keep him out of Gavin's reach. "You son of a bitch!" he shouted, "You give me that kid, right now!"

"Mr. Hawley, please," I said, dancing around in a circle while trying to get him to listen to reason. "Look, your wife is obviously in no condition to be taking care of a child, and you shouldn't have to be burdened with it..."

"I'll burden you!" he yelled, and swung a ham-sized fist at my head, but I ducked it. I was more afraid he'd manage to hit the child than me, for I'd been a boxer in my younger days and knew how to take a punch, but it was at that moment that we were suddenly joined by several other people.

Five

Clark Rodgers had gotten back to his office only a few minutes after I'd left, and Mike had told him what I'd had to say about Maisy. He'd also mentioned that I was asking about the child, and it took Clark all of thirty seconds to figure out where to find me, so he'd called the sheriff's office and arranged for a deputy to meet him at Gavin's place — Long Creek is outside of his jurisdiction — and then rushed out to try, as he explained to me later, "to keep Gavin Hawley from forcing us to find a new Santa before Saturday, since the one we had would be laid up with a bunch of broken bones!"

At that moment, however, I was glad to see them, because they pulled Gavin away from me and the deputy held him back while Clark began to apologize to him for my interference, but Gavin wasn't listening.

"I want you," he said, "to arrest that bastard for trespass, and lock him up in the jail! He ain't got no right to come in here and tell me how to raise my grandkid!"

"Clark, as a Minister, it's my duty to report child abuse when I know of it! I didn't trespass, because Mrs. Hawley opened the door and invited me in. And when I heard the boy screaming, I came into the room to make sure he was okay, and I'm pretty sure a court would clear me of any wrongdoing on that score! I'm making an official recommendation that this child be removed from this home, because he's suffering abuse and neglect at the hands of his grandfather and this — this child bride of his!"

Clark grabbed me by the arm and dragged me out of the room, still holding the boy, and hustled me down the stairs to the kitchen. I was protesting that we had to do something for the child, but he kept telling me to shut up, so finally I did.

As we entered the kitchen, the deputy followed, but Gavin and Tiffany Hawley went into some other part of the house, to my surprise. The deputy came over to us and said, "Clark, this guy's right; that kid don't belong here. I already called Family Services in, they oughta be here in ten minutes or so."

Clark nodded at him, still holding on to my arm. "Yeah, Bob," he said, "I'm with you on that. I just need to have a talk with Dex here, okay?"

The deputy nodded and walked away. A second sheriff's car pulled in just then, and a female deputy came inside and asked if the child I was holding was the one that Family Services was called about. Clark said he was, and she took him from me as an ambulance came into the driveway. The paramedics were sent, it seemed, to make sure the child wasn't harmed, and would look for any signs of actual physical abuse.

Clark got my attention and looked me in the eye. "Now, you listen to me, and you listen good, Dex! I didn't want to let Gavin have the boy last night, but he was next of kin, so there wasn't anything I could do at that moment. The only good thing to come out of your nosiness is that we can get FS involved now, and get the boy away from that bastard and his druggie wife! The problem is that by storming into his house, you ran the risk of getting yourself shot, and it would have been his word against yours whether he had the right to shoot you or not. And how much weight do you think your word would carry if you were dead? We've been after Gavin for years, and all you're gonna do is mess up a long term investigation..." He suddenly trailed off, as he realized he was saying too much. "Look, forget you heard that!" he said. "Dex, you just gotta stay out of this, okay?"

Clark spent the next fifteen minutes lecturing me, and finally calmed down. The Family Services people showed up about then, and Clark told me to get on my bike and go home. "And don't worry about Gavin and his trespass charges, I'll get him chilled out over that. You just go home, Dex, and stay out of this whole mess, okay?"

I nodded and got on the Harley. The snow was still falling, and the road was wet, but nothing was sticking or freezing, so I could handle it.

There's something about a cold ride that makes you think, and I did a lot of it as I rode back into town. I could admit to myself that I was the overly curious sort, but maybe Clark was right, and the last thing I should be doing was sticking my nose into a police investigation, and a murder investigation at that! What was wrong with me? I wasn't the kind to do this sort of thing, or at least, I never had been — unless you count that whole confession-obsession thing, and that was just a matter of wondering who had told me what. Heck, according to some Priests I knew, they suffered from it too, so it couldn't be that big a deal, right?

I went home and let myself in, and Baggins informed me that I'd been gone long enough for him to need a treat to celebrate my return. I got down the little box of treats I always kept for him and shook a few into my hand, then sat down in my favorite chair and let him jump up on my lap.

He settled himself and contentedly ate the treats right out of my hand, purring the entire time, and I found myself wishing I could find that state of mind that would allow me to purr with contentment.

Unfortunately, that was a gift that God only bestowed upon cats, and was one of the many reasons why some cultures have thought cats must be some form of deity, or the favored pets of deity. I sighed instead, and set Baggins down so that I could have a cup of fire cider to take the chill out of my old bones.

I had an appointment with three of the ladies from the parade committee at two, so I thought about making myself a light lunch and then decided to go eat in town, instead. I called Norma Kelly, one of the ladies I was to meet with, and asked her if the three of them might want to join me for lunch at the Diner, and she giggled like a schoolgirl as she said she was sure they'd all love to. I left it to her to call the others, and began the process of bundling up for the ride into town.

I already had on a pair of long johns, with a pair of heavy Levi's and a big flannel shirt over them, but now I added a thick fleece jacket, then covered that with the long, leather duster that went almost to the floor. The flaps that hung down around my feet had straps to anchor them to my ankles, which kept them from getting into the spokes of my wheels, and I topped it all off with a leather pilot's cap, the kind with the ear flaps that come down and fasten under your chin. That kept my ears from freezing off as the cold wind rushed by them, and since I was rather fond of my ears, I considered it a necessity.

I was the first to arrive at the Diner, but Norma showed up a few minutes later, and she had Letha Waters and Betty Miller, who happened to be Mike the cop's mother, with her. I stood as I greeted the ladies and we all sat at the big round table near the front of the place. That suited me fine, since it was right in front of the window and I could keep an eye on the Harley as we ate.

Aw, c'mon, it's a '48 Panhead! Do you know how many guys would steal a bike like that, just to be able to say they had ridden one? I didn't let her out of my sight very often, and even then only if there was no way I could help it.

"Dexter, it's so nice of you to offer to buy us lunch," Letha said, and I smiled.

"It's my pleasure," I said. "I was thinking about lunch and about our appointment, and I thought I'd see if we couldn't just combine the two."

"Well, it's certainly sweet of you," Betty added. "I don't get to eat out often, so this is quite a treat, and with the most charming man in town!"

I blushed and smiled, making the ladies happy. Each of them was single—Letha and Betty were widows, and Norma's husband had run off with his secretary ten years earlier, and all three were around my age, so they'd all made it plain that they'd be willing to entertain me as a suitor. Somehow, I had managed to avoid any entanglements so far, and I wanted to keep it that way. I never willingly met with any one woman alone, so that none of them might get the idea that I was favoring one over another. I still missed Nervy, and there were many reasons why I didn't want to marry again, or at least not anytime soon.

"Thank you," I said, "but let's get our orders in and then we can talk business. Everyone know what you want?" Since almost everyone in town ate at the Diner now and then, we all knew the menu, so it didn't take long to let the waitress know what we wanted. I ordered the rib eye steak, a favorite of mine, while the ladies all went for the special of the day, which was Yankee Pot Roast. Once we'd gotten the sweet tea we'd all asked for, I offered to let Miss Norma take the floor.

"Well, Dex," she said, "we just wanted to get together with you and make sure that everything is ready for the parade. I mean, is the suit fitted and everything? Do you have enough padding for it? Is there anything else we need to address?"

I smiled and winked. "Well," I said, "padding isn't a problem, I come with plenty of that already built in." I slapped my ample belly to emphasize the point, and all three ladies tittered. "The suit will be a perfect fit, I'm sure, and I can't for the life of me think of anything else that might need to be done to get me ready. I'm pretty sure it's all been taken care of, to be honest."

Letha grinned. "All that padding is from eating your own cooking," she said. "Now, if you had a good woman to cook for you, you'd be in a lot better shape!"

"Oh, I don't know," I said with a forced laugh. "Nervy was a fine cook, and I got pretty well padded a long time ago. I think maybe it's just that God thinks I need to play Santa, so he's got me in character all the time, don't you?"

Betty reached over and patted my arm. "And he couldn't have chosen a better person for the job," she said. "Dexter, this town has come to life since you came here, I do declare. Why, last year we couldn't find anyone to do half the things that you volunteer for, like playing Santa for the kids, or helping out with the youth at church the way you do."

"Oh, it's all my pleasure," I said, wondering how I could get them off the subject—and then it hit me. "Right now, I just feel so bad for that poor young woman who was murdered last night, don't you? Did any of you know her very well?"

Three sets of eyes rolled as one, and I knew I'd hit the jackpot in my search for information. If you really want to know something about someone in a small town, find the local gossip circle and ask an innocent question, then sit back and enjoy the ride!

"Well," Letha said, "that was Brenda Hawley, you know. Oh, she was always a wild one, she was, and always in trouble of one sort or another when she was a girl. Her mother took off when she was only four, bless her heart, and that father of hers was probably the worst kind of parent she could have had. He's rich, and it seems like he thought the way to take care of his daughter was to just give her whatever she wanted."

"Lord, yes," Betty chimed in, "she was spoiled rotten, she was, then she took off for the city when she was only eighteen, about ten years ago. She went to New York and tried to make it as an actress, but she ended up coming back here. I hear tell she was just living in one of her daddy's rent houses, and supposed to be writing a book, but all I seen was her livin' off her daddy's money again."

Norma tsk'ed. "Now, she wasn't that bad, and none of us ought speak ill of the dead. Since she had that little boy, Colton, she's actually settled herself down a lot. She was going to church now and then over in Harrison, I heard someone say, and I was glad of it. A child that little needs a grounding in the Gospel, you know."

Letha nodded. "That's true, since Colton was born, she turned over a whole new leaf. She took good care of that child, I can say that for sure."

I nodded with them, and leaned forward. "Yeah, and he's an adorable kid. Seems a shame, him not having a daddy who could come and take him. Do you think anyone around here knows who the father is?"

All three of them looked at one another, but they all seemed genuinely unaware of the father's identity. It was Letha who spoke up first.

"I don't think anyone knows for sure," she said, "but it's no secret that she was quite friendly for some time with her next-door neighbor. I can't think of his name at the moment, but I know he's a single man who runs an accounting business from his home."

"So, he's an accountant, then?" I asked.

Norma nodded. "Yes, but I'm afraid that's about all I know. As to whether or not he's the little boy's father, I couldn't say, and I don't think anyone else knows either."

I shrugged, as if it were not of any importance to me. "Oh, well," I said, "I just think it would be nice if the boy had a father to turn to."

Six

For the rest of the day, it seemed like every time I turned around I ran into Clark. Needless to say, that made it very difficult to "stick my nose" into anything, so I ended up spending most of the day at home. I curled up on my couch with a cup of fire cider spiced coffee, Baggins on my lap and one of my favorite Terry Pratchett novels in hand, and just let myself relax. I had a fairly light schedule for the following day, which was a Wednesday. That was one of the days I was scheduled to offer counseling at the county detention center, and I needed to be out there before nine a.m.

Baggins, being the perfect alarm clock, woke me promptly at seven with his usual kneading of the tender flesh on my chest. I had gotten smart enough to wear a heavy shirt to bed every night, especially now that the weather was cooling off, so the awakening wasn't quite as unpleasant as it used to be. I scratched him behind his ears, making him purr, then set him on the floor as I got to my feet. We did our usual morning dance to the kitchen, with me making a stop in the bathroom along the way. By the time I caught up with him, he was doing his figure eights around the bowl.

I decided to surprise the cat, and got down a can of his absolute favorite food. When the can opener began singing its song, poor Baggins was just about to have a heart attack with excitement, but when I used a fork to get the food into his bowl, and set the bowl back on the floor, I thought that cat was going to bow down and worship me.

After two cups of spiced coffee, I felt myself ready to face the winter world that awaited me outside, and began bundling up and preparing for the ride through the chilly air. A glance at the thermometer outside my kitchen window told me that we were getting close to freezing, so I added an extra layer of thermals under the jeans, just to be safe. Now, as long as it didn't snow or rain, I should be just fine.

The detention center is about fifteen miles away from where I live, on the other side of Harrison. It's one of those new, modern looking jail type buildings, with lots of tall fences around it and enough concertina wire to make it look like some sort of old military prison. Anyone who tried to climb over those fences would find themselves fileted like a fish, I was sure. Fortunately, no one had tried it since it was built about twenty years ago.

As always, when arriving at the detention center, I checked in with the duty Lieutenant and let him know I was there. He smiled and hooked a finger at me to tell me that he wanted to speak to me for a moment. I went into his office and sat down in the chair in front of his desk, then waited to see what he needed.

"Dex," he said, "just wanted to ask you how it's been going. You having any problems, anything I can help with?"

"No," I said, shaking my head. "I've actually been getting a pretty good response from most of your inmates, or at least none of them have been openly hostile toward me. Have there been any complaints coming back to you about me?"

The lieutenant shrugged and made a face that I thought was rather comical. "The only complaint I have heard is that you can be a little bit long winded on some of your sermons," he said, "but any preacher who doesn't get that complaint from time to time probably isn't doing his job, right?"

I nodded and chuckled. "So true," I said. "Maybe I should try to stretch it out a few minutes longer, you think?"

He laughed. "Might be a good idea, maybe some of them would actually get the message. Listen, I just want you to know how much we appreciate your efforts in here. My wife gets a kick out of the fact that some of the people who have gotten out of the jail have been showing up at our church, and trust me, that's all because of you."

I smiled, but shook my head. "No, Lieutenant, believe me on this," I said. "If any of these men are finding their way back to Jesus, it's not because of me. I only carry the message, but it's the Holy Ghost who has to call them to hear it. This is God's doing, not mine, and I don't want to try to take credit for His work."

The lieutenant grinned, and I nodded as I left his office. I slapped down the pride that tried to rise at his words, and simply whispered a prayer of thanks for God's wonderful blessings as I made my way to the little visiting room that they let me use for individual counseling sessions.

The room had a small table and only two chairs, all three of which were bolted to the floor. It was normally used by attorneys visiting with a client, and was designed for one-on-one meetings. That worked perfectly for me, since that's how I dealt with counseling sessions, one on one. On this particular morning, I had only five sessions scheduled.

Ironically, my very first scheduled session was with Enzo Mallozzi, whose nickname was, of all things, Beans. He had told me that he got the nickname because he was an accountant, a "bean counter," as they say, but it didn't take me long to realize that it probably had more to do with the fact that he had a constant problem with flatulence. Unfortunately, a staple of jailhouse food tends to be, you guessed it, beans; poor Beans couldn't possibly escape his problem as long as his diet consisted primarily of beans, pasta and a lot of boiled cabbage. I steeled myself for the olfactory tragedy that was about to happen to me, and told the guard to go ahead and bring him in.

"Beans," I said as I rose to shake his hand. "How have you been?"

"Ah, not bad," he said in reply, his grip firm in my hand. "Good to see you again, Chappy. World treatin' you okay?"

"Oh, I can't complain," I said, "and no one would listen if I did. So, what can I do for you today?"

Beans smiled as he took the seat across from me. "Listen, Chappy, I was wondering if you could try to talk to the judge for me. I know, I know, you can't do anything about my sentence, and he probably won't either. I fudged the paperwork, so now I gotta do the time, I understand that, and I got no beef with that. The thing is, they got me in the general population here, and I got people trying to make me do stuff for them that could get me in even more trouble. So, I'm thinkin', maybe you talk to the judge, and he moves me into one of the private cells they got upstairs, the ones they save for the big shots. Think you could do that for me, Chappy?"

Beans was a local guy, and his Italian mobster act was literally just that, an act. I knew people who had gone to school with him in Harrison, and they assured me that he didn't have this Sicilian accent until after he saw the movie Scarface. I didn't call him on it simply because I didn't want to embarrass him, so I grinned and told him I would see what I could do.

As I said, though, Beans is a local guy. As a local accountant, he would know just about everyone in the business, so I asked him if he might know an accountant who lived on Blevins Street, just off of Cemetery Road in Alpena, and he smiled like a fox who had just caught a chicken dinner.

"Preston Gotter," he said. "About as straight an arrow as you'll ever run across. Most accountants, you wanna know how to fudge your tax returns, they'll find a way to do it for you, but not Gotter. Won't even talk about it; you either do things the honest way, or you go someplace else. Why you askin'?"

I carefully told Beans a short and somewhat cleaned up version of events, adding that Gotter may have been seen slipping away from Brenda's place a few times at night. He grinned again.

"Maybe," he said. "Gotter's a lonely type, and word was he had some secret girlfriend for a while, so maybe it was Brenda, who knows? And she wasn't bad lookin', either, and she was a nice person the last few years. It's a shame she got iced like that, but if you're thinkin' Gotter mighta done it, Chappy, think again. I don't think the guy could hurt a fly." He screwed up his face, then. "You want my guess, if someone whacked Brenda, it was probably somebody connected with that daddy of hers. Old man Hawley's dirty, sure as sin, he uses that construction company to launder

49

money for a lot of, let's just say, less legit operations he's got his fingers into, know what I mean?"

I nodded. "I gotcha," I said. "Thanks for filling me in, okay? And do me a favor, and keep your ears open; if you hear anything else that might be important, let me know. You've got my number, and all you have to do is say you're having a crisis and I can come and see you anytime as the jail Chaplain."

Beans grinned and said he'd see what else he could find out. Some of the people he was in with would know people on the street, and would hear things that he could pick up on. I was hoping someone might have heard who killed a young woman a couple nights back, and might let it slip in front of Beans.

The rest of my sessions went by pretty quickly, most of them having more to do with minor marital issues than anything else. I was happy to offer the advice I could, and as chaplain, I was allowed to take messages from inmates to spouses, as long as I logged them with the lieutenant on duty. I did so as I was leaving, showing him the festive drawings that a few of the inmates were sending to wives and children, and he smiled.

"Chappy," he said, "I'll grant you that it's God behind it all, but you've made an incredible difference in some of these men. Keep it up, man."

Once again, I had to fight down the pride as I left.

When I got outside, I got my phone out of the saddlebag — you're not allowed to take them inside the jail, of course — and googled up the number for Preston Gotter. I called immediately, and asked for an appointment to discuss my taxes, and what I might need to do to be sure they were filed properly early next year. Gotter said he would have time to see me the following day, if I could be there by ten, and I assured him that would be perfectly fine by me.

Meanwhile, it was Wednesday, and just happened to be the day of the last monthly flea market of this year. I decided to see if Crazy Maisy had set up her stall like she usually did, because I was getting low on fire cider and, if I were to be honest, I was just a little more than curious about that woman.

I love going to the market, and especially at Christmas time. I had discovered it the year before, not long after I had moved here, and before my hair had gotten long enough for people to start referring to me as Santa. This year, however, just about everyone that I met there that day called out, "Merry Christmas, Santa!" as I walked by, so I greeted them all with a hearty "Ho, ho, ho, Merry Christmas," and I got such a kick out of the children present, staring at me in awe as parents hastily explained that Santa only wore the red suit on Christmas Eve, or when he was making special appearances.

I spotted Maisy, and could tell that she was doing a brisk business so I waited until she had a quiet moment. When she finally looked around at me, I smiled and said, "Merry Christmas, Maisy," but she simply glared at me and said, "Oh, the Noise! Noise! Noise! Noise!"

Naturally, I recognized the line: How the Grinch Stole Christmas was a story every parent knew, and every grandparent had better know. I had read it to Chance many times when he was a child, and got to read it to Ben for the first time just the year before. I grinned at Maisy and said, "Maybe Christmas — perhaps — means a little bit more."

51

She continued to simply glare at me, but didn't say another word so I picked up a bottle of the cider and a couple of handmade catnip pillows for Baggins. "Well," I said, "I went by Brenda's house and took a look, and the man you saw sneaking away from her place seems to have been her neighbor, as you guessed. He's an accountant, and a single man; could be they just were friends, don't you think?"

"Bah, and a humbug to go with it," she said. "Friends don't sneak through the hedges! Clark Rodgers and a deputy sheriff already been out to my place to see me, and they trampled my herb garden while they was at it."

I grimaced; I'd known when I went to the police that they'd end up talking to her, but there was no help for it. "Sorry about that, but I'm sure they had to verify the story you told me about seeing someone sneaking away from Brenda's house. Of course, they had to talk to you. How much damage did they do? I'd be willing to pay for it."

She'd been looking at some of her stock, but suddenly spun her head and let one eye focus clearly on me. The other eye was mostly closed, but there was a hint of a smile on her lips. "Ye don't need to pay nothin'," she said. "That deputy told me how ye went out there and made a stink at Hawley's place and got that poor boy away from his crazy, drunk, degenerate grandfather. That's what I meant, when I said I knowed ye was a good man. Ye done the right thing, even when it got them in power agin ye!"

"Well, for what it's worth, I'm going to see that neighbor tomorrow. I made an appointment to discuss my taxes with him, but I'm really just out to get a feel for the type of person he is. To be honest, I've heard some good things about him, and at least one person who knows him doesn't believe he could possibly have hurt Brenda."

Maisie grinned. "Mayhap he didn't," she said, "but seems t'me if they was friends good enough for sneakin' through hedges, then might be they was friends good enough to be watchin' each other's place, wouldn't ye think? Could be he seen something, but could be he's afraid to tell."

I chewed on my cheek for a moment, thinking about what she was saying. She could be absolutely right. If Gotter was close to Brenda, he might well know something even if he himself were not guilty. And, let's face it, many people would be afraid to come forward after witnessing a murder. There had been too many stories about killers not being arrested, and then coming after the witnesses who spoke against them.

I grinned. "You know," I said, "you're a whole lot smarter than you let people think you are."

She suddenly lifted a hand to her face and pushed back the wild locks of hair that usually hung in front of her eyes, and winked at me. "I'm a mite prettier than I let on, too," she said, and it hit me that Maisy wasn't nearly as old as I had thought she was. I smiled and dipped my head once in acknowledgment that she was correct, and then asked, "Any chance you know anything else interesting about Brenda?"

She shook her head. "Nah," she said. "Stupid girl wouldn't even speak to me after I told her I wouldn't help her get herself knocked up. Guess she was mad at me, but they's only two reasons why a single woman wants to be pregnant. Either she's tryin' to trap a man, or she thinks so little of herself that she's cravin' the only one she thinks could ever truly love her, and that'd be a baby of her very own."

I'd had to deal with female soldiers who had low self-esteem, and I knew that she was correct on the second part. As for using pregnancy to trap a man, I was fully aware, having counseled many a young soldier to demand a paternity test before agreeing to either marriage or child support, that this was a ploy as old as mankind. As far as I knew, the only man who never had to wonder if the child was his, at least for a moment now and then, would've been Adam.

And me, of course.

Seven

There really wasn't much more for me and Maisy to talk about, but I wasn't ready to go home yet. It had warmed up considerably since morning, and I was regretting the extra pair of thermal underwear, but I decided to wander around the market for a bit. I picked up a few fresh greenhouse veggies, carrots and celery that I love to munch on, and bought a bag of taffy from the candy stall. I was just about to decide to head for home when my phone rang in my pocket.

When I answered, I got the recording that said it was a call from the county detention center, so I pressed five when prompted to accept the call. I always accepted calls from the detention center, even though they were collect calls, because there was no way to know whether it could be a potential suicide on the other end of the line.

This time it wasn't, it was Beans. "Hello, Beans," I said once the call was put through.

"Okay, Chappy, you asked me to let you know if I heard anything. I got somethin', don't know if it's what you want or not, but thought I'd better tell you, anyway. You know that builder guy we were talking about a while ago?"

Of course, I realized he was talking about Hawley, so I grunted an acknowledgment.

"Well, he's got this little cutie, y'know? And she really, really likes, um, candy, y'know? Well, turns out the builder is footing the bill for the candy, but the cutie is shoppin' for more than candy at the candy store, you get me?"

I got him, all right, and was disgusted when I realized that he was telling me that Hawley was supplying the money for his wife's drug habit, and that she was having an affair with the drug dealer. Beans said that was all he had, so I thanked him, but I couldn't see how it fit into Brenda's death. To me, it just didn't seem connected.

I gathered up all of my purchases, and headed for the Harley in the parking lot. At least, while I was riding down the road in this cool air, my legs weren't going to sweat themselves to death in the double thermals. I went home and relaxed, and even managed to resist the temptation to try the new bottle of fire cider, finishing off the old one first.

I got to Gotter's house about twenty minutes early the next morning, anxious to meet the man and get my own sense of who he was. I knocked on the door, but there was no reply, so I wondered if he was outside somewhere, and wandered around to the back of the house in search of him. I spotted a shed with an open door, and heard what sounded like whistling coming from it so I walked over to it and stuck my head inside.

I found him, leaning over a table inside the shed, so I smiled and said, "Hello!"

He turned around to face me, and my heart almost jumped into my throat! He was wearing an apron that was covered in blood, and was holding a bloodied filet knife! For a long moment, I was sure I was about to die, as I thought of the fact that this was the type of knife that must have killed Brenda — but then I glanced at the table he'd been leaning over and realized the man was actually cleaning fish.

I concentrated on getting my heart rate back down where it belonged, while Gotter stammered and apologized.

"Oh, you must be Chaplain Merriman," he said. "I am so sorry, I got up early and went down to the creek to do some fishing, and I was hoping to get these cleaned and fileted before you got here. I'm so sorry, I must look awful."

I waved a hand in dismissal. "No, no, no apologies are necessary. I'm actually rather early, I guess I'm just the impatient sort. I can come back in a little while, let you get finished up."

He wouldn't hear it. Instead, he showed me into his office and asked me to wait just a moment while he went to wash up. He put the rest of the fish on ice as we left the shed, assuring me that he could come back and finish them in a little while.

When he came back to the office, I actually learned quite a lot about tax-preparation and why having an accountant do my taxes, rather than one of the services you could find in department stores, was a good idea, so I really did sign on as a client with him. While all I had was my pension for income, he had shown me that there were many ways that I could take advantage of perfectly legitimate deductions and drastically reduce the amount of tax that I would have to pay. Like any other American, I was more than happy to hear about paying less taxes.

Once we were done with business, I sort of indicated Brenda's house next door with my head and asked him if he knew her, explaining that I'd been the one to find her when she stumbled into the road. I had wondered if I would be able to get him to talk about her at all; ten minutes later, I was wondering if he would ever shut up.

"Oh, my goodness," he said, "yes, I knew her quite well. She and her little boy, oh my goodness, I loved them to pieces. For a little while there, I had actually wondered if he was mine, the boy I mean, because we had a relationship for several months after she first came back to town, but it finally dawned on us that we're better friends than lovers." He looked a bit sheepish, and grinned at me. "It's a little embarrassing, but I just couldn't keep up with her, you know, in the bedroom. She was into a few things that I had just never even known existed, and I just couldn't get into them. Don't get me wrong, it's not like she was into anything weird, or kinky, not really, but..." He shrugged. "I guess I'm just a prude," he said at last.

I managed to laugh it off, wondering how to bring up the fact that he'd been seen sneaking through the bushes on the night of the murder, when he brought it up, himself.

"What's really odd," he said, "is that I can't help wondering if maybe I could've saved her. See, for the last few weeks I've had the feeling that maybe she was interested in trying again, maybe there was hope for us, and if it meant I had to, you know, accept a few things, well, I could do that. I mean, I'm a big boy, right? So anyway, night before last I went over to try to talk to her about it, and see if I was right, but when I got there I could hear her talking to someone inside. I wasn't sure what to do, so I figured I would just wait. I mean, I didn't want to embarrass her, or myself, for that matter. So I just came on home, and ended up going to bed early. I didn't know anything was wrong until the police lights were flashing all around her house, and it woke me up." He fell silent for a moment, and I saw tears slide down his cheeks. "It sort of sounded like she was arguing with someone about something, and now I just can't help thinking that if I'd only knocked, she might still be alive."

I reached over and patted him on the shoulder. "Preston," I asked, having reached a first name basis earlier in our meeting, "why didn't you go to the front door? Why sneak around to the back?"

He didn't seem to wonder how I knew about that but laughed, an ironic laugh that said he was asking himself the same question. "The police asked me that," he said. "They came to see me yesterday, and asked about it, and I'll tell you the same thing I told them. We'd gotten in the habit, back when we were actually in a relationship, of going through the back doors of each other's houses, just so we wouldn't cause talk with the other neighbors. The ones on the other side of her place are a nice older couple, but they'd have been shocked if they knew she was letting me in like that, so we just figured it was best to keep it quiet. Even after we ended that, we still, whenever we needed to talk or anything, we always used the back doors. I guess it was just familiarity. The cops said there was enough obvious wear on the footpath between our houses to back up my story, and they didn't consider me a suspect because they didn't find any sign of my fingerprints anywhere in the kitchen, which is obviously where she was killed."

I sat there and looked at him for a moment. "Preston, do you have any idea who she might have been arguing with? Or what it might have been about?"

Gotter shook his head. "No, not a clue. I didn't even think to look and see if there was a car in her driveway, because that would have meant going around to the front. You can't see our driveways from the back; the view is blocked by trees. I thought maybe—but I shouldn't speculate, not on something like this."

I caught his eye and asked, "What? Preston, if you think you know something, tell me. It could be important."

He shrugged, and then gave me a weak smile. "Well, I did wonder if it might have been her father she was arguing with. I know she told me just last week that his new wife was costing him a fortune in drug bills, and she felt like the woman was snorting up her son's inheritance, not to mention her own. She was pretty ticked over it, and I thought maybe that would be the person she'd most likely be fighting with."

I thanked him, and then left a moment later. I could think of one other person she might argue with about that same subject, though, and that would be her tiny blonde stepmother! Could it be that Tiffany Hawley had killed Brenda to prevent her from raising a stink over the money Gavin was blowing on her?

Eight

It seemed to me that I needed to find out more about Mr. and Mrs. Hawley, but I didn't know how I was likely to do that without making a stink, especially after my last go round with them. Still, I've always been the kind to take the bull by the horns, so I rode out to Long Creek again, and the big estate with that barn shaped mansion on it. I stopped at the intersection to let a semi-truck pass before I turned into the road the house fronted on, and glanced over at the mansion.

Suddenly, the front door opened, and a young man stepped out with Tiffany Hawley on his heels. She was smiling from ear to ear, and when the man turned toward her, she slipped her arms around his neck and kissed him passionately, then stood there smiling and being coquettish as he got into a powerful sports car and drove away, down the road in the opposite direction from me.

A split second later, I was following the car from a distance, staying far enough back that he probably wouldn't even notice a motorcycle on the road behind him. We went straight ahead for about four miles, and then it hit me where he was going, as he pulled in at the main office and equipment yards of Hawley Construction.

The young man parked his car and walked into the brick office building that was probably worth more than any home twice its size, and I didn't even hesitate. That crazy curiosity of mine wanted to know what was about to go down between these two, so I walked into the building just as boldly as the youngster had.

There was no one in the reception area, so I stood there and listened for a moment, then heard some voices growing louder and heated. I followed the sound, and a moment later I could make out what was being said.

"Ten thousand," the young man was saying. "That's how much you owe me, Hawley, and I want my freakin' money!"

"Stone, you're outa your mind! I told you two weeks ago I wasn't paying for her crap anymore, and to cut her off, and then we settled up. I don't owe you squat, and I want you to stay away from me, and stay the hell away from my wife! You may think I don't know what's been going on, but you forget something, Sonny boy—I've been around a lot longer than you have, and I know all about how things work. You saw my pretty little wife, and you got her to put out so you'll keep bringing her dope, but then you want me to pay for it, too? You're a stupid punk, boy, and I..."

There was a crash, and Gavin Hawley let out a strangled scream. I didn't think, but just pushed my way through the door and looked around it. Stone, who was obviously the drug dealer Beans had told me about, had Hawley by the throat, and when I yelled, "Hey!" he spun around and shoved something into his pocket. Was it a knife? And was it possibly a folding filet knife?

Stone glared at me, and shoved his way out past me, mumbling something about getting my fat you know what out of his way. I almost went after him, but Hawley looked like he was actually gasping for breath, so I wanted to be sure he was okay before I left there. I went over to him and asked him if was all right, and he looked up at me. It took a second, but then he said, "Yeah, I guess I am — thanks to you. I think that boy woulda killed me if you hadn't come in when you did."

"Yeah, well, I actually was wanting to talk with you, but when I heard the yelling, and then it sounded like you were in trouble, I thought I should just come on and make sure everything was on the up and up, in here."

Hawley nodded. "Glad you did," he said. He looked up at me. "The other day, you said you're a — what was it, a preacher?"

"I'm a US Army Chaplain, retired," I said. "I'm still a Minister, just sort of a freelancer, nowadays."

He looked at me for a long moment without saying a word, then asked me to have a seat. "I've needed to talk to somebody," he said, "so I guess it might as well be you."

I was slightly surprised, but then again, I'd seen many people come to a point where they just needed to let something out, and I guess it's part of the calling God placed on me that I'm one that people can talk to. I took the chair on my side of his desk, and said, "Mr. Hawley, are you a Christian?"

Hawley sat there for a moment and then smiled. "I think I was once," he said, "but that was a long time ago. I used to go to church every Sunday, when I was young, and I even — nobody would ever believe it, today, but I wanted to be a preacher, once. Isn't it strange, how we can go so far from where we started out? It doesn't really seem like life is long enough for so many changes, does it?"

I nodded. "Sometimes, I think you're absolutely right. I know I've come a long, long way from where I was when God first called me."

Hawley didn't say anything for another few seconds, and then he sniffled as a tear made its way down his cheek. "I've made so many mistakes," he said. "I've had a lot of chances to do the right thing, and let 'em all slip right through my fingers. I lost my wife years ago 'cause I couldn't be the husband I should've been, always chasin' women and never home where I should be. Then I lost my daughter 'cause I didn't know how to be any kind of father to her. She ran off to New York City, wanted to become a movie star, she said, but the people up there said she didn't have it in her. They told her she had a great imagination and oughta be a writer, so after five years she asked me could she come home and use one of my rent houses, and I said okay. Hell, I didn't know what else to say, y'know?"

I nodded slowly. "I'm a father," I said. "I think I can understand how inadequate you felt to deal with her, and why you felt you could only give her what she wanted. However, what children need isn't so much our constant consent to be who they want to be, they need our guidance to help them become who they need to be."

He was nodding his head, but there was an anger in it. "Yes, yes, I know," he said, "and I know that I failed her — but we had found a way to make amends between us. She came to see me a couple of weeks ago, and we had it out, talked things through. We came to some agreements, and I put a stop to a lot of my wife's spending, and then set up a trust fund for Brenda to use in taking care of my grandson. Tiffany was pissed, but she was bleeding me dry with wanting this and wanting that, but — ah, hell, there's nothin' to really say, is there? Brenda's gone, and I can't bring her back, and there's so much crap goin' on that I can't even stay sober long enough to keep my grandson." He wiped away the tears that were now flowing freely, and then looked at me again. "I was so mad at you the other day, when they took Colton from me, but the shape I've been in, you were right to make 'em do it. If that boy had stayed with me and Tiffany, there's no telling what might have happened to him."

I smiled at him. "That only proves that you do have a good heart, Mr. Hawley," I said. "You're putting your grandson's welfare before your own desires. That's one of the marks of love, that you put someone else before yourself, just as Jesus gave His own life as the sacrifice for all of us, so that we can be free of the guilt of our sins."

Hawley looked at me. "I'll be honest," he said, "I don't know that I'm ready to go back to church just yet. I've still got a lot I need to figure out, and I don't know what's gonna happen about other things that are goin' on. But I'll tell you this," he said. "When it comes time, I'll be sure to talk to you."

I smiled, and said, "Anytime, Mr. Hawley. Although, I do have one question I'd like to ask you now, if I may?" He shrugged, and I felt a twinge of guilt because I knew the question I was going to ask wasn't one he was expecting. "Would you know who Colton's father is?" I asked.

He sat there and looked at me for a moment, and then shook his head slowly. "No," he said softly. "She absolutely refused to tell me, even after we made peace. She said I wouldn't understand, and would make trouble."

A contractor that he worked with came in then, and suddenly I knew that our moment of camaraderie was over. I thanked him for his time, and he nodded curtly, so I let myself out and got onto the Harley. I rode home, and actually felt that I'd accomplished something; just the fact that Hawley was willing to even discuss things calmly was a miracle in my book, and if I had planted a seed that might bring him back to Jesus, then so much the better.

I rode home and was welcomed by Baggins, who wanted to repeat the evening before and spend it curled up in my lap. I told him we'd talk about that after I found myself some dinner, and was eying my options—chicken noodle soup or chili, both of which came in a can—when the doorbell rang.

I should mention that of the few people who ever come to visit me, almost none of them ever use the front door. For that doorbell to ring usually means one of three things: it's an official visitor, like a tax collector or cop; it's someone who's trying to find Annie Wilson, the lady whose estate sold the house to Nervy and me, and who wrote a series of novels that were so popular that people were still trying to track her down for an autograph eight years after her death; or the school was making the kids sell candy bars to raise money again, and every parent in town figured I'd be a soft touch for their kid to hit since I obviously ate a lot. For the first, I tried not to be home, for the second I tried to convince them that there was a better book they should be reading anyway, and for the latter—well, I bought a lot of candy once or twice a year.

This particular time was the oddball, though, for when I opened the door there was no cop, no book fan and no candy bar; there was Naoma Brodrick, and she was holding my freshly altered Santa Suit.

"Naoma," I said, "hello! You didn't have to bring the suit out here, I could have come by and picked it up tomorrow."

She smiled and handed it to me. "Oh, I don't mind," she said, and to be honest, Dex, there was something I needed to talk to you about, anyway."

"Well, then come on in," I said, and took her coat as she entered. I have a nice coat closet just inside the door, and hung it there. "Can I offer you something to drink?"

"Well, maybe something warm," she said with a grin, and I told her I knew just the thing. I had found that a shot of fire cider in some hot chocolate was wonderful on chilly nights, and a few moments later, I had made a new convert and had been forced to tell her where to buy the brew.

"Okay," I said when we were sitting at the table sipping our spicy cocoa, "so what did you need to talk to me about?" I prepared myself for just about anything, since I'd found that a lot of the people I'd come to know in town seemed to think I was easier to talk to than even Brother Freddy, but I wasn't prepared for what she had to say. Naoma Brodrick knocked me right off my chair with the first words out of her mouth.

"Dex," she said, looking at me pleadingly. "Dex, my husband Keith is Colton Hawley's father."

Nine

"Whoa," I said, "slow down and run that by me again?"

She nodded. "You heard it right," she said. "They had an affair four years ago, and when she got pregnant, she said she didn't want or need any kind of support from him because she had plenty from her father. They ended the affair and Keith only got to see Colton when he could slip away from me, but about six months ago, when Brenda's father married that little tramp, he cut Brenda off, and she ended up needing help after all. She asked Keith, and that's when he confessed everything to me." Her eyes were moist, and I could tell she was still struggling with the emotions involved, but she said, "It took me a month, but I got past the hurt and forgave them both. I'm a Christian woman, and it was the right thing to do, so we went and sat down with her and talked it all out. The past few months, we've even been having them over from time to time, and sometimes Brenda would let Colton stay over with our own three girls. They all get along great, and little Colton is a delightful boy who is so much like Keith that I'm just thrilled to have him around when he can be."

I sat there for a few moments, just staring at her. "Naoma, why are you telling me this?" I asked.

She smiled sadly. "Dex, no one else knows about this. As far as anyone knew, even the children, Brenda and I had become friends, and that's why we took such an interest in her and her son, and there really is some truth in that. One of the things that I give thanks to God for every day since she died is that the weekend before, she stayed with us, and I was able to lead her to the Lord. I miss her already, but at least I know I'll see her again one day, in Heaven, and so will little Colton." She looked at her nails, and then back up to my face. "Dex, Keith and I talked it over, and we know he's going to have to come forward. That's his son, and he should be with us, not some foster family in the state system, where he could be abused or worse. We know you've been asking questions about Brenda's death, that's all over town — some people have taken to calling you 'Father Dowling,' for goodness sake, after the old TV show!" She chuckled at that, and reached over to pat my hand. "Anyway, we just wanted you to know that we loved Brenda, and had no reason to hurt her. We both know what people are likely to think, once Keith steps forward, and he's planning to go and see the Police Chief tomorrow. We — well, we were sort of hoping you might go with him?"

I smiled and laid my free hand atop the one she still had on my other one. "Naoma, I'd be glad to," I said. "What time?"

She let a tear of what I thought must be relief slip out of her eye, and said, "Thank you, Dex. Say about ten a.m.? We can just meet you at the station, if you want."

I nodded. "I'll be there," I said, and then I helped her on with her coat and said goodnight.

Once she was gone, I began thinking through everything I'd learned, and wondering how it all fit together. The way I saw it, there were five distinct possibilities, which I'll present here in no particular order:

The first possibility was that Gavin Hawley lost his temper and killed his daughter. After all, I had only his word that they'd made up. For all I knew, he could be a stone cold liar and a murderer as well.

Second, it could be that Tiffany Hawley and her drug dealer boyfriend tried to shake Brenda down for money after Gavin closed the purse strings. Brenda would certainly have refused, which could lead to a fight, and potentially a killing.

Then there was Preston Gotter. He admitted thinking she wanted him back, and going to her house the night of her death to ask her about it. What if he had actually gotten to speak with her, but she laughed in his face? More than one seemingly mild-mannered man had gone into a rage at the thought of humiliation in front of a woman he obsessed over. Just because police didn't find his prints in the kitchen didn't mean a thing; he might well have gone home, gotten his favorite filet knife, and gone back to do the deed. Heck, he may have put on the big rubber gloves he was wearing when I saw him cleaning the fish.

Fourth, Keith Brodrick, assuming he really is Colton's father, might have killed Brenda to keep the secret of his love child from getting out, or maybe to avoid paying child support, or — though I couldn't imagine it, not really — it was even possible that Naoma might have done it, for the same reasons, or maybe just out of pure jealousy that her husband had been with another woman.

And of course, the fifth possibility was that I didn't have a clue what I was talking about, and the killer was someone else altogether. I went over it and over it, but couldn't come to any real conclusions about any of my suspects, so I finally took Baggins' advice, got the book out and headed for the couch.

Friday morning, the day before the parade. I had a meeting with the parade committee at the community building at noon, but I'd promised to meet Keith and Naoma at the Police Station at ten, so I fed the cat, made the coffee and spiced the living dickens out of it, climbed into long johns and everything else and slipped away from home at around eight thirty. I figured I had time to go by the Diner and have breakfast—they had steak and eggs for the breakfast special on Fridays—and I rode up and parked on the side of the building by where the dumpster sat waiting for all the trash that would accumulate over the weekend.

There was someone digging in the dumpster as I shut off the Harley and climbed off, and I recognized Bo, from the trash truck. "Hey," I said, "how's it going?"

He looked around and smiled. "Oh, hi," he said. "Goin' okay, how about you?"

"Pretty good," I replied. "You, uh, you're really into your job, there, I see."

He glanced down to where he was holding a stack of cardboard boxes that he'd cut down and flattened. "Oh, nah," he said. "I just know they get a lot of cardboard here, and if I stop by and cut it down before it gets to be too big a pile, it holds more, so I do that for 'em." He cut down another one as I started to turn away, then called out, "Oh, hey, did you ever find your toys?"

One of the reasons that you should never tell a lie, not even a little white lie, is because you have to always remember every little white lie you've told, so that no one catches you in one of them. I wasn't exactly your consummate liar, and had already forgotten that I'd told that little white lie about trying to find the toys that Brenda was supposed to donate, so I turned to him and went, "Huh?" with an amazingly stupid look on my face.

Luckily for me, though, Bo wasn't the brightest bulb in the pack, either, and didn't catch my gaff. "The toys that lady was supposed to donate for the kids, for Christmas?" he clarified, and I recalled my fib. I smiled as if I'd just understood what he was saying, and shook my head. "No, I'm afraid we didn't. Just bad luck on that, I guess, eh?"

He smiled ruefully. "Yeah," he said, "no kidding! If she was donating any of her kid's old toys, you might have had a real haul. That toy Corvette she's got in the house must've cost at least a thousand bucks!" He shook his head again and reached into the dumpster for another box, and I glanced at the knife in his hand.

It was a long, thin filet knife, and it suddenly dawned on me that he'd had it in its scabbard when I'd seen him the other day, as well. Suddenly all the things he'd said ran through my mind: "...she was such a sweetheart..." "...real shame, her getting stabbed to death in her own kitchen like that..."

I had listened to the radio reports that morning, too, and it suddenly hit me that not once did the announcer ever say she was stabbed to death in her kitchen; they'd only said she had died as the result of multiple stab wounds. And a person would have to be in the house to know about the toy car.

"Hey, you okay?" the guy asked me, and I raised my eyes from his knife to his face. Instant realization dawned on him, and he knew I'd figured it out. He looked around and realized the very same thing I did — there was no one in sight, absolutely no one who could come to my aid.

He spun and lunged at me, the knife thrust out to take me right through the ribs. A thin blade like that, held at a low angle, would slip right between them, and would either puncture my heart or my lung, possibly even both. Either way, if he managed to get that blade into me, I was a goner within seconds, and we both knew it. I dodged, my old boxing skills coming back like the ability to ride a bicycle, and we danced there in the alley.

The problem is that he was half my age and in a whole lot better shape than I was. He was also fast with that knife, and whenever I tried to get a punch in, he lunged at me again. I could either keep myself covered and out of his reach, or I could strike out at him, but not both, so I took a chance and tried to take him down fast. I poured all two hundred and sixty pounds of myself into one wild roundhouse punch that caught his jaw even as the knife stabbed into my side, but all that weight managed to send him reeling into slumberland, and the knife only sunk in a couple of inches before he fell and pulled it back out.

Still, it hurt, and I mean it hurt bad! I caught myself falling from the pain and shock, and I fumbled for my phone to call for help, but I couldn't find it. I knew that if I passed out, and Bo came to before I did, I was dead, so I did the only thing I could think of.

I prayed.

When I was in Seminary School, one of my professors, whose name was Jenkins, loved to tell the story of when Paul and Silas were going to preach at Philippi, and encountered a girl who was possessed by an evil spirit. Being men of God, they cast out the demon, but as it turned out, there were certain men who used the girl and her evil spirit to predict the future, and make themselves wealthy. When it was gone, they were angry, so Paul and Silas were beaten and cast into a prison cell. Late that night, however, they both felt the need to praise God, and begin to sing and shout His Praises, and as the Bible tells the story, while they were singing and shouting, the whole prison began to shake and tremble, and the doors all flew open, and Paul and Silas could have walked out—but they stayed there, so that when the guard came to check on them and found that they had refused to escape when they had the chance, he ended up giving his life to Jesus Christ.

The moral of the story, according to Professor Jenkins, was simple: whenever you stop fooling around and really start to pray, God's going to rock your world!

At that moment, that story came back to me, and I prayed with all of my heart that God would send someone out to put trash in the dumpster and find me. I prayed that if it was his will that I die and be taken home that day, that somehow my death would be used to bring a blessing to someone, even if it only meant that this killer would be caught, and as I was praying, and beginning to fade away, I suddenly felt the whole world begin to shake, and suddenly there was a noise like an earthquake, and I knew that God was rocking my world right then and there!

Ten

I came to in the back of an ambulance, and looked up to see a number of familiar faces. There was Clark Rodgers, and Mike Miller, and just about everyone else I knew in Alpena. I saw Gavin Hawley standing outside, and several others I recognized. The paramedics had an oxygen mask on my face, and I pulled it off. I looked up at Clark and croaked out, "There was another man..."

Clark nodded. "Bo Bennet," he said. "We got him, Dex. He was layin' there out cold right next to you, and seein' as how you'd obviously been stabbed with that skinny little filet knife he was carrying, it didn't take me but a second to figure out why you and he were dukin' it out. He killed Brenda, didn't he?"

I nodded. "Yes," I said. "I almost missed it, but then God let me run into him again, and I caught his mistake. He knew that Brenda had been killed in her kitchen, even though it hadn't been in the news report that morning, and he knew about Colton's toy Corvette in the house, so when I put that together with the kind of knife he carried, I knew. He knew I'd made him, and wanted to shut me up, but I used to box a bit..."

Clark laughed. "I'll just bet you did," he said. "Paramedic says his jaw is broke in at least three places. How many times did you hit him?"

"Just the once," I heard someone behind me say, and I swiveled my head around to see Crazy Maisy sitting in the ambulance with me. "Well, I seen it," she said, "ye didn't hit him but the once! Was all it took, too!"

The paramedic leaned over and shined a light into my eyes, and asked me my name, age and where I lived. When he was satisfied I wasn't delirious, he said, "Dex, you've got what amounts to a minor flesh wound, but that knife was pretty nasty, so I've started you on some IV antibiotics. We're gonna take you to the hospital for observation overnight..."

"Wait a minute," I said. "Minor flesh wound? He shoved that thing right through me, I felt it!"

The paramedic, who happened to be Letha Waters' oldest daughter Becky, looked at me like I was a drama queen. "Oh, puh-leeze," she said. "Yeah, you got stuck with it, but only about two inches of it got you. Dex, you've got about ten inches of fat there, between your skin and anything critical, so yeah, it's not that big a deal except for the risk of infection. Now, we're taking you in overnight for observation..."

"Oh, no, you're not," I said. "I'm Santa in the parade tomorrow, and there is no way I'm gonna miss out on that! Now, you can patch me up and I'll go see Doc Jackson for a good shot of penicillin or whatever, but I am not missing that parade!"

Becky scowled. "You're nuts," she said, but she took out a phone and called Doctor Jackson, who was a local physician, and he agreed to see me as soon as I could get there. Becky said the ambulance couldn't take me there, but Keith and Naoma Brodrick suddenly stepped up and offered to drive me. I climbed carefully up off the cart, and managed to get onto my feet and stand, then remembered something.

"Hey," I said. "Just before I passed out, there was some really big noise, and it seemed like the whole world was shaking. What was that?"

Everyone sort of looked around at one another, but no one knew what I was talking about, so I started to think maybe it was something God did just for me, to let me know that help was on the way—but then I saw Maisy's grin. "Maisy? Do you know what it was?"

Suddenly most of the people there started laughing, and Clark Rodgers said, "Oh, that? There was a noise, all right, and I guess if you were right under it, it mighta seemed like the world was shaking. Maisy, here, was coming to town, she said, and something told her to come look behind the Diner, and she found you laying there with blood all over the place, so she grabbed a board and started bangin' away on the side of the building, screamin' her fool head off that somebody had killed you! Everyone inside thought she'd gone nuts, so they called me, and I came across the street and found you and Bo, like we said. Wasn't no earthquake, it was just Crazy Maisy!"

I looked over at Maisy and smiled, and she seemed to blush a bit under all that wild, unkempt hair. I leaned close to her, and said, "Maisy, remember the other day, when you said you didn't really believe in God?" She scowled, but she nodded. "Well, let me tell you something—I sure am glad that God believes in you. Whether you know it or not, Maisy, He sent you as an answer to my prayers."

She ducked her face and seemed to actually preen just a bit, as if she was proud of herself, even if she didn't know what had really happened. I wasn't fooled, though; that was only what she wanted the others there to see, wanted them to think. As for me, she peeked up once from under her hair, and winked, and I knew that she wasn't preening for pride. She was preening for me.

"Miss Maisy," I said solemnly, "I shall be riding in a sleigh float in the parade tomorrow, dressed as Santa Claus. Would you consider accompanying me on that ride?"

I could see the startled expressions on the faces of Naoma, Letha and Norma, as I made that offer without even consulting the parade committee, but I stared them all down. Maisy blushed and preened a bit more, then looked up at with both eyes open and grinned from ear to ear.

"Yep," she said, "I'd be right glad to! See, Santa I believe in!"

The whole crowd burst into laughter, and Naoma asked Maisy if she'd like to ride along with me to the doctor's office.

"Reckon as I ought," she said. "Lordy knows somebody's gon' have to take care of him next few days!"

I suddenly wondered if I was ever going to be free of Maisy, but I should have known better. She wasn't one who would ever want to settle down, I was sure, but I wasn't fool enough to turn down her offer of help while I recovered.

I'm pretty sure Nervy would've liked Crazy Maisy.

Doc Jackson gave me a couple of holy cow that hurts shots in my rump, added about a half dozen stitches and said that as long as I took it easy for the next week or so, I should be fine, so I got Billy Kelly—there are a lot of Kelly's in Alpena—to ride my Harley home for me, and let Keith and Naoma drive me and Maisy on home to my place. She helped me inside, and got me settled on the couch for a recuperative nap. A bit later she woke me to tell me that my bath water was ready, and when I opened my eyes, I thought for a moment I was dreaming, for she had taken a bath of her own, and was wearing one of my shirts as a dress.

"I's washin' my clothes," she said, "and hope that's all right with ye. And yer bathtub looked so invitin' I just had to give it a try."

It was perfectly fine with me, and I was absolutely delighted with the transformed Maisy who stood before me. I'd known she wasn't as old as I was, nor even as old as some thought her to be, but when she had clean hair that was neatly combed, and wasn't wearing old clothes that were too big for her, she was actually a rather attractive lady, and probably a good ten or twelve years my junior. Having her in the sleigh tomorrow would be a Christmas Surprise for the whole town, I was sure!

I got my bath, and then Maisy helped me to my bed and I slept most of the rest of the day away. I think Doc put something into those shots to make me sleep a lot, that day, to be honest, but it definitely helped. When I got up the next morning, I was refreshed, and ready to put out my best, "Merry Christmas!" and "Ho, ho, ho," performance yet!

Keith and Naoma came to pick us up, and I could tell they were both surprised at Maisy, but I was delighted to see that they had Colton with them.

"After you caught the killer," Keith said, "I told Chief Rodgers that I was Colton's father, and we produced the paternity test we'd gotten done when I came clean to Naoma about it, just to be certain. He got Judge Bailey on the phone and set up an emergency hearing, and we were granted temporary custody of Colton, pending a final hearing next month."

I hugged them both, wincing as I did so. "That is wonderful," I said. "I know Colton is going to have a rough time for a while, but at least he knows now who you are. How did your girls take the news?"

Naoma laughed. "Them? They're overjoyed! They now have a brother to pick on, and they've already gotten started!"

"That trash man was arrested, and after a couple of hours of being questioned, he confessed to killing Brenda," Keith told me. "Seems he'd had a real thing for her, and went to her house the other night to tell her about it, drunk and out of his mind. When she rejected him, he just went berserk, and stabbed her over and over. When he left, he said she was still on the floor, and he thought she was dead already, but somehow she got up and ran out where you found her. If she hadn't, little Colton would have found her in the morning, Dex. That would've been awful."

Later that day, I learned that Tiffany and her drug dealer boyfriend had also been arrested, charged with possession of drugs and with extortion, because they were actually trying to blackmail Gavin Hawley, threatening to turn him in if he didn't cough up more money. He beat them to the punch, putting all of his assets into a trust fund, and then turning himself in to the sheriff and confessing to fraud on some of his construction jobs, and his confession about money laundering would be taking down a few well known Arkansas politicians.

That morning, though, since Colton was all taken care of, all I cared about was the parade. With a little help, I managed to get into the Santa Suit in the back room of the fire department, and climb up onto the big sleigh that was actually sitting on a flatbed trailer. Maisy got up there beside me, smiling widely. There were some huge bags of candy on the floor, and we began tossing it out to the children of Alpena and the surrounding towns, who were lining the street with their parents.

As we passed the Citgo Station, I spotted Colton, sitting up on Keith Brodrick's shoulders, and motioned for Keith to bring him to me. The boy hadn't seen me in the suit before, and was overwhelmed that Santa actually knew his name, but he went into happy fits when he realized he got to ride with us for the rest of the parade. He laughed like mad as he helped us throw candy, and was having a wonderful time, but as the parade drew to a close, I could tell the sadness was setting in. I pulled him onto my lap and asked him what was wrong, wondering what he would say, and praying that God would give me the right words to say in response.

He sat there for a long moment, and then he looked up into my eyes. "If I tell you a wish, will it come true?" he asked.

"Sometimes," I said.

He stared into my eyes for another moment, and then he said, "I wish my Mommy was here."

I pulled him close to me and held him tight, then I pointed up at the sky. "Do you know who lives up there?" I asked him, and he nodded.

"God lives up there," he said, "cause that's Heaven."

"That's right," I said, "but someone else lives up there now, too."

He looked at me for a moment, then looked up at the sky again. "Mommy?" he asked.

"Yes," I said, "so even though your Mommy isn't here right now, she's watching you, and I'm sure she's very, very proud of you!"

The little boy looked back at me once more, and then raised his eyes to Heaven. He sat there for a moment before lifting his hand in a slight wave and whispering, "Hi, Mommy. I love you." Turning to me he added, "I love you too, Santa...and God as well."

Then I was so choked up I could hardly get the words out. "God loves you right back, Colton, and so do I. Merry, merry Christmas little man."

If you enjoyed this story, please leave a review. Your words really mean a lot.

Get a **FREE** *unpublished* cozy mystery story and be among the first to hear about Liz's new book releases and special deals when you join her email list here:

http://lizdodwell.com/signup/

By Liz Dodwell:

Doggone Christmas
A Polly Parrett Cozy Mystery

Captain Finn Treasure Mysteries:
The Mystery of the One-Armed Man (Book 1)
Black Bart is Dead (Book 2)
The Gold Doubloon Mystery (Book 3)
The Game's a Foot (Book 4)
Captain Finn Boxed Set (Books 1-3)

For you coloring enthusiasts, take a look at Liz's publication Christmas Mandalas and Messages Adult Coloring Book.

Liz Dodwell devotes her time to writing and publishing from the home she shares with husband, Alex and a host of rescued dogs and cats, collectively known as "the kids." She will tell you, "I gladly suffer the luxury of working from home where I'm with my "kids," can toss in a load of laundry in between radio interviews, writing, editing, general office work or baking pupcakes (dog treats) while still in my PJs. I love what I do and know how lucky I am to be able to do it. Oh, and if you asked me what my hobbies are, I'd probably say reading murder mysteries, drinking champagne, romantic dinners with my husband and yodeling (just joking about that last one)."

Jacob Lee joins Liz in their first collaboration of the Chaplain Merriman series.